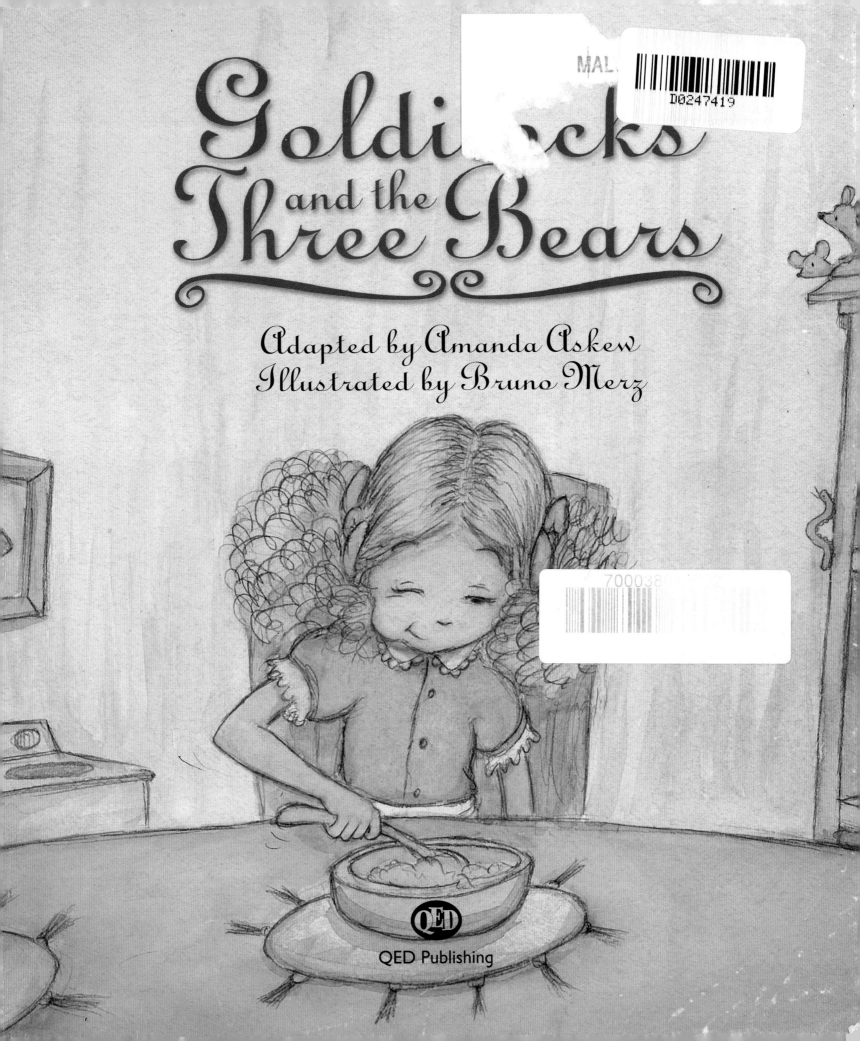

Goldilocks
and the
Three Bears

Adapted by Amanda Askew
Illustrated by Bruno Merz

QED Publishing

One day, a little girl called Goldilocks went for a walk in the forest.

She came upon a house and knocked on the door. When no one answered, Goldilocks went inside.

At the table in the kitchen, there were three bowls of porridge. Goldilocks was hungry.

She tasted the porridge from the first bowl.

"This porridge is too hot!" she exclaimed.

Then, she tasted the porridge from the second bowl.

"This porridge is too cold!" she cried.

Finally, she tasted the last bowl of porridge.

"Ahhh, this porridge is just right," and with that, she ate it all up.

After she'd eaten the porridge,
Goldilocks went into the living
room where she saw three chairs.

She started to feel a little tired.

Goldilocks sat in the first chair to rest her feet.

"This chair is too hard!" she exclaimed.

Then, she sat in the second chair.

"This chair is too big!" she whined.

Finally, she tried the last and smallest chair.

"Ahhh, this chair is just right," she sighed.

Just as she settled down into the chair to rest, it broke into pieces.

Goldilocks wanted to rest,
so she decided to try
the bedroom.

She lay in the first bed, but it was too hard.

Then, she lay in the second bed, but it was too soft.

Lastly, she lay in the third bed and
it was just right.

Goldilocks fell asleep.

As she was sleeping, the three bears came home.

They went into the kitchen, and what did they see?

"Someone's been eating my porridge," growled Papa Bear.

"Someone's been eating my porridge," said Mama Bear.

"Someone's been eating my porridge, and they've eaten it all up!" cried Baby Bear.

Next, the three bears went into the living room and what did they see?

"Someone's been sitting in my chair," growled Papa Bear.

"Someone's been sitting in my chair," said Mama Bear.

"Someone's been sitting in my chair and they've broken it to pieces," cried Baby Bear.

The three bears began to look around and when they reached the bedroom, what did they see?

"Someone's been sleeping in my bed," growled Papa Bear.

"Someone's been sleeping in my bed," said Mama Bear.

"Someone's been sleeping in my bed, and she's still there!" cried Baby Bear.

Just then, Goldilocks woke up and saw the three bears.
The bears didn't look very happy.

"Help!" Goldilocks screamed.

She jumped up and ran out of the room.

Goldilocks ran out the door and into
the forest. Never again did she go
wandering in the forest near the home
of the three bears.

Notes for parents and teachers

- Look at the front cover of the book together. Can the children guess what the story might be about? Read the title together. Does this give them more of a clue?

- When the children first read the story or you read it together, can they guess what might happen in the end?

- What do the children think of the characters? Is Goldilocks kind? What about the three bears? Who is their favourite character and why?

- The three bears are an animal family that act like humans. Can the children think of any other stories with similar characters?

- When the bears arrive home, do the children think they will find Goldilocks? What do the children think the bears should have done to Goldilocks?

- The bears eat porridge. What do the children like to eat? Would they eat their favourite meal at a table? Ask the children to draw or paint their ideal eating experience.

- What other endings can the children think of? Perhaps the children can act out the story, and then the new endings.

- By eating the bears' porridge and breaking the chair, Goldilocks acts selfishly. What other acts can the children think of that are selfish?

Copyright © QED Publishing 2010

First published in the UK in 2010 by
QED Publishing
A Quarto Group Company
226 City Road
London ECIV 2TT
www.qed-publishing.co.uk

ISBN 978 1 84835 486 9

Printed in China

A catalogue record for this book is available from the British Library.

Editor: Amanda Askew
Designers: Vida and Luke Kelly